TURN ON THE NIGHT

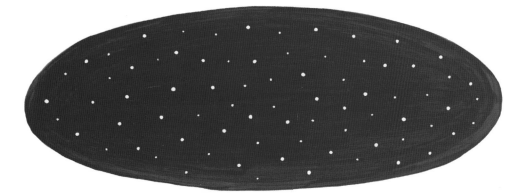

GERALDO VALÉRIO

GROUNDWOOD BOOKS / HOUSE OF ANANSI PRESS

TORONTO BERKELEY

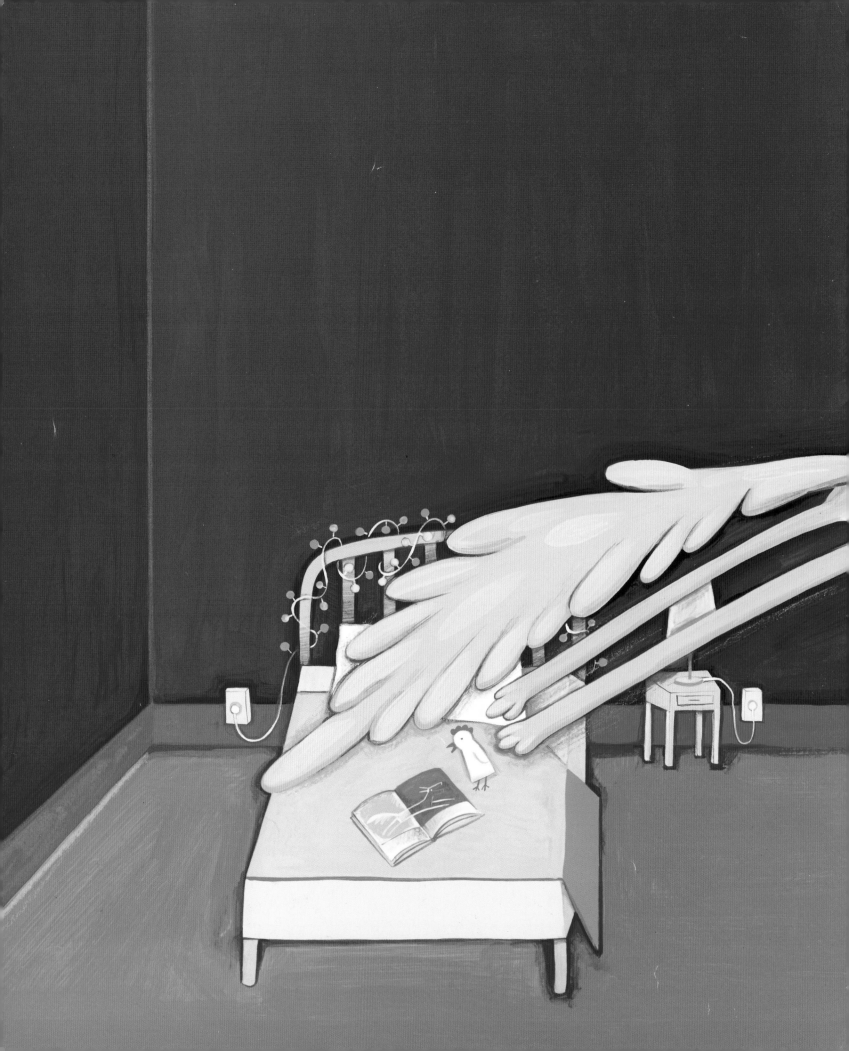

For Dora and Stela

Groundwood Books / House of Anansi Press
groundwoodbooks.com

We acknowledge for their financial support of our publishing program the Canada Council for the Arts, the Ontario Arts Council and the Government of Canada.

Canada Council   Conseil des Arts
for the Arts   du Canada

ONTARIO ARTS COUNCIL
CONSEIL DES ARTS DE L'ONTARIO
an Ontario government agency
un organisme du gouvernement de l'Ontario

With the participation of the Government of Canada
Avec la participation du gouvernement du Canada | Canada

Library and Archives Canada Cataloguing in Publication
Valério, Geraldo, author, illustrator
Turn on the night / Geraldo Valério.
Issued in print and electronic formats.
ISBN 978-1-55498-841-9 (bound).—ISBN 978-1-55498-842-6 (pdf)
I. Title.
PS8643.A422T87 2016   jC813'.6   C2015-908434-2
C2015-908435-0

The illustrations were created with acrylic paint and color pencil on paper.
Design by Michael Solomon
Printed and bound in Malaysia

MIX
Paper from
responsible sources
FSC® C012700